MR. SLOW

by Roger Hargreaves

WORLD INTERNATIONAL

Mr Slow, as you might well know, or maybe you don't, lived next door to Mr Busy.

He'd built his house himself.

Slowly.

It had taken him ten years!

And, as you might well know, or maybe you don't, Mr Slow talked in an extraordinarily slow way.

He . . . talked . . . like . . . this.

And every single thing he did was as slow as the way he talked.

For instance.

If Mr Slow was writing this book about himself, you wouldn't be able to read it yet.

He wouldn't even have got as far as this page!

For instance.

If Mr Slow was eating a currant cake for tea, it took him until bedtime.

He'd eat it crumb by crumb, currant by currant, chewing each crumb and each currant one hundred times.

For instance.

Last Christmas, it took Mr Slow until New Year's Day to open his Christmas presents.

And then it took him until Easter to write his thank-you letters!

Oh, he was a slow man.

Now, this story isn't about the time Mr Slow went on a picnic with Mr Busy.

That's another story.

No, this story is about the time Mr Slow decided to get a job.

He read all the job advertisements in the Sunday paper (which took him until Wednesday) and then he went and got himself a job reading the news on television.

Can you imagine?

It was very embarrassing!

"Good . . . evening . . .," said Mr Slow. "Here . . . is . . . the . . . nine . . . o' . . . clock . . . news."

It took him until midnight to read it!

And everybody who was watching went to sleep.

So, that job wasn't any good.

Was it?

Then, Mr Slow got himself a job as a taxi driver.

"Take me to the railway station," cried Mr Uppity, as he leapt into his taxi. "I have a train to catch at 3 o'clock!"

"Right . . . ho," said Mr Slow, and set off.

At one mile an hour!

And arrived at the station at 4 o'clock.

So, that job wasn't any good.

Was it?

And, that summer, Mr Slow got a job making ice cream. But, by the time he'd made the ice cream, it wasn't exactly the right sort of weather to be selling ice cream!

Brrr!

So, Mr Slow got himself a job making woolly scarves. But, by the time he'd finished making the scarves, it wasn't exactly the right sort of weather to be selling scarves!

Phew!

Poor Mr Slow.

He went around to ask the other Mr Men what he should do.

"Be a racing driver!" suggested Mr Silly.

Can you imagine?

No!

"Be an engine driver!" suggested Mr Funny.

Can you imagine?

No! No!

"Be a speedboat driver!" suggested Mr Tickle.

Can you imagine?

No! No! No!

But then, Mr Happy had an extremely good idea.

Most sensible.

"Be a steamroller driver," he suggested.

And today that is exactly what Mr Slow does.

Slowly backwards and slowly forwards he drives.

Up and down.

Down and up.

Ever so slowly.

The next time you see a steamroller doing that, look and see if Mr Slow is driving it.

If he is, you shout to him, "Hello, Mr Slow! Are you having a nice time?"

And he'll wave, and shout back to you.

"Yes . . . thank . . . you . . .," he'll shout.

"Good . . . bye!"

MORE SPECIAL OFFERS
FOR MR MEN AND LITTLE MISS READERS

In every Mr Men and Little Miss book like this one, <u>and now</u> in the Mr Men sticker and activity books, you will find a special token. Collect six tokens and we will send you a gift of your choice
Choose either a <u>Mr Men</u> or <u>Little Miss</u> poster, **or** a Mr Men or Little Miss **double sided** full colour bedroom door hanger.

Return this page **with six tokens per gift required** to:
Marketing Dept., MM / LM, World International Ltd.,
PO Box 7, Manchester, M19 2HD

Your name:_____ Age: _____

Address: _____

_____

_____Postcode: _____

Parent / Guardian Name (Please Print)_____

Please tape a 20p coin to your request to cover part post and package cost

I enclose <u>six</u> tokens per gift, and 20p please send me:-

Posters:-   Mr Men Poster   ☐ Little Miss Poster ☐

Door Hangers - Mr Nosey / Muddle ☐   Mr Greedy / Lazy ☐

     Mr Tickle / Grumpy ☐   Mr Slow / Busy ☐

20p   Mr Messy / Quiet ☐   Mr Perfect / Forgetful ☐

     L Miss Fun / Late ☐   L Miss Helpful / Tidy ☐

     L Miss Busy / Brainy ☐   L Miss Star / Fun ☐

Stick 20p here please

Please Tick Appropriate Box

We may occasionally wish to advise you of other Mr Men gifts.
If you would rather we didn't please tick this box ☐

|← 100 mm →|

250 mm

ENTRANCE FEE 3 SAUSAGES

MR. GREEDY

Collect six of these tokens
You will find one inside every
Mr Men and Little Miss book
which has this special offer.

1
TOKEN

Offer open to residents of UK, Channel Isles and Ireland only

NEW

Full colour Mr Men and Little Miss Library Presentation Cases in durable, wipe clean plastic.

In response to the many thousands of requests for the above, we are delighted to advise that these are now available direct from ourselves,
for only £4.99 (inc VAT) plus 50p p&p.
The full colour boxes accommodate each complete library. They have an integral carrying handle as well as a neat stay closed fastener.
Please do not send cash in the post. Cheques should be made payable to **World International Ltd. for the sum of £5.49** (inc p&p) per box.

Please note books are not included.

Please return this page with your cheque, stating below which presentation box you would like, to:
Mr Men Office, World International
PO Box 7, Manchester, M19 2HD

Your name:_____

Address: _____

_____

_____Postcode: _____

Name of Parent/Guardian (please print):_____

Signature:_____

I enclose a cheque for £_____ made payable to World International Ltd.,

Please send me a Mr Men Presentation Box ☐

              Little Miss Presentation Box ☐

(please tick or write in quantity)
and allow 28 days for delivery

Thank you

Offer applies to UK, Eire & Channel Isles only